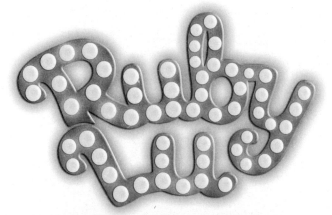

STAR of the SHOW

Also by Lenore Look

Ruby Lu, Brave and True
Ruby Lu, Empress of Everything

STAR of the SHOW

by
Lenore Look

illustrated by Stef Choi

Atheneum Books for Young Readers
New York   London   Toronto   Sydney

ATHENEUM BOOKS FOR YOUNG READERS

An imprint of Simon & Schuster Children's Publishing Division
1230 Avenue of the Americas, New York, New York 10020
ATHENEUM BOOKS FOR YOUNG READERS is a registered trademark of
Simon & Schuster, Inc.
For information about special discounts for bulk purchases,
please contact Simon & Schuster Special Sales at 1-866-506-1949
or business@simonandschuster.com.
The Simon & Schuster Speakers Bureau can bring authors to your
live event. For more information or to book an event, contact the
Simon & Schuster Speakers Bureau at 1-866-248-3049
or visit our website at www.simonspeakers.com.
Book design by Lauren Rille
The text for this book is set in Lomba Book.
The illustrations for this book are rendered with pencil and shaded digitally.
Manufactured in the United States of America
0411 FFG

10 9 8 7 6 5 4 3 2
Library of Congress Cataloging-in-Publication Data
Look, Lenore.
Ruby Lu, star of the show / Lenore Look ; illustrated by Stef Choi.
p. cm.
Summary: Ruby Lu's father loses his job on her first day of third grade,
which causes many things in her life to change, and she is willing to do a lot
to help out but giving up some things seems impossible.
ISBN 978-1-4169-1775-5 (hc)
[1. Unemployment—Fiction. 2. Conduct of life—Fiction. 3. Family life—Fiction.
4. Schools—Fiction. 5. Dogs—Fiction. 6. Chinese Americans—Fiction.] I. Choi, Stef, ill.
II. Title.
PZ7.L8682Ruk 2012
[Fic]—dc22
2010009927
ISBN 978-1-4424-2040-3 (eBook)

To Charity and Madison,
the brightest stars in my sky
—L. L.

To Tony,
my sunshine
—S. C.

"These dark days will be worth all they cost us
if they teach us that our true destiny is not
to be ministered unto but to minister to ourselves
and to our fellow men."

—Franklin D. Roosevelt,
First Inaugural Address, March 4, 1933

"Isn't it funny that something as bright as a star
spends all its time in the dark?"

—JonArno Lawson,
Poet Extraordinaire of Canada, July 28, 2010

CHAPTER ONE
The Best Thing About Third Grade

The best thing about third grade was absolutely everything.

"Waffles with berries and extra whipped cream!" Ruby exclaimed. Ruby liked the breakfast.

"Hooray!" exclaimed her cousin Flying Duck in Chinese Sign Language. Both girls wiggled their thumbs, which means "thank you" in CSL.

Ruby's dad wiggled his thumbs back. Unlike other days when he would rush off to work before anyone else made it downstairs, he was in the kitchen serving his Back-to-School Breakfast Special for the girls. It was a tradition that he had started when Ruby was in kindergarten.

"The key to a good school year is a good breakfast," said Ruby's dad, slipping a waffle in front of her.

"And the key to a good meeting with your boss," added Ruby, giving her dad a wink, and digging right in.

Ruby's dad winked back. She could tell that he was impressed that she remembered that he had an important meeting with his boss. "Third graders sure know everything!" he said cheerfully.

"And they eat pretty fast too," said Ruby, gobbling down the last of her waffle.

"Mee too!" said Oscar, stuffing his cheeks. Ruby laughed. He was her baby brother, and he was so silly and hungry *all* the time.

"Take it easy," Ruby said to Oscar. "You're not going to school yet, you're only going to day care."

Ruby's mom, who usually stayed home with Oscar, was out with Flying Duck's parents, helping them look for work. Flying Duck's parents, who had recently moved from China, needed to find jobs, and Ruby's mom, who was good at speaking Cantonese and English, was translating for them. So it was decided that Oscar, who was almost one, would go to day care three mornings a week.

Ruby gave Oscar a kiss on the head. "You'll have a great time!" she said, lean-
ing carefully away from
Oscar's sticky high chair
and even stickier hands.

"Kisssssssssss you,"
said Oscar, blowing
Ruby a kiss.

Flying Duck also gave Oscar a kiss on the head, and Oscar, quick as a Venus flytrap, caught Flying Duck with a whipped-cream hug.

Then Elvis, Ruby's new dog, jumped up and covered Flying Duck with kisses, licking off the sweet, fluffy cream that Oscar had smeared on her.

"Oh you silly dog," said Ruby, throwing her arms around Elvis and rubbing her face into his fur. "I'm going to miss you today."

"Urrrrrr?" said Elvis. He was the best thing that happened to Ruby during the summer. One day he appeared on her doorstep, and by the end of the summer, she had adopted him. And now he was the absolute best thing about third grade. Ruby was looking forward to taking him to dog obedience school for the first time, after school. He was full-grown and had some unusual skills for a dog, such as yoga, riding a bicycle, and balancing plates and balls on his head, but obeying Ruby was not one of them. He had a mind and life of his own. He was always

practicing his Down Dog position . . . or his Cobra . . . or his Spider. But he never came when called, or sat or begged or heeled like a normal dog. This was frustrating to Ruby, but she loved him just the

same. His best skills, Ruby felt, were the most important ones—giving Ruby a listening ear whenever she needed it, and watching TV with her. He loved TV, especially animal shows, and so did Ruby. Nevertheless, she could hardly wait to train him to do some normal dog tricks.

"Guess where we're going after school today?" Ruby asked.

Elvis looked at Ruby with round wet eyes.

And Ruby looked at Elvis.

"Owwwwwww," moaned Elvis sadly. He seemed to say that he was going to miss Ruby terribly until she got home.

Ruby swallowed.

"Oh, I wish I could bring him to school with me," she said, squeezing Elvis.

"You'll be taking him to dog school soon enough," said Ruby's dad.

"Okay," said Ruby, wiping a tear from her eye.

Ruby threw her arms around her dad and gave him a kiss. "Bye, Daddy," she said. "I love you."

"I love you too, Ruby," he said, giving her a hug.

Then she and Flying Duck hurried out of the house and down 20th Avenue South toward third grade.

CHAPTER TWO
A Cloud Drifted By That Looked
Like a Dog

Third grade was in the big kids' hallway. Fourth and fifth graders, who looked as important as teenagers, brushed by Ruby on their way to class. Colorful posters covered the walls, inviting students to all the clubs.

Ruby could hardly wait to join them all.

Ruby liked her new classroom. An alphabet banner circled the top of the room in *cursive* letters. A fish tank bubbled in the corner. The floor was as shiny as ice. And lo and behold, Ruby's name was on her desk—in cursive!

Ruby slipped right in. It was bigger than a second-grade desk, Ruby thought, and definitely

much bigger than a kindergarten desk. A bigger desk meant Ruby was bigger. And she was. She was now the height of one upright vacuum cleaner.

Ruby thought about all the exciting things that third graders got to do. You learned to play the recorder. You could join the third-grade recorder orchestra. You could get a job helping in the library, or passing out milk in the cafeteria. You could even become famous if you won the Third-Grade Haiku Competition at the end of the year. Everyone was looking forward to it. There was a ceremony and prizes. Best of all, there was applause. Ruby loved applause.

But that was not all.

Ruby was looking forward, most of all, to learning Spanish. A Mexican family had moved into the neighborhood, and their son, Panchito, was a bit ornery. He didn't like anything or anyone. He didn't like school. He didn't like basketball. He didn't even like candy. He never went into Fred's candy store, but stood outside every day after school while everyone else went in. He spoke English, but he spoke Spanish better. Ruby thought that if she learned a little Spanish, she could help him feel more at home.

"*Hola*," Ruby said, saying hello in Spanish, as she swung her feet under her desk. A few heads turned. Ruby had tried to teach herself Spanish from her father's CD, *Teach Yourself Spanish in Twenty-five Easy Lessons*. But it wasn't easy. The rest of the CD was *moong-cha-cha*, which in Chinese means confusing, not clear, or fuzzy in the head.

"*Moong-cha-cha*," Ruby whispered. A few more heads turned. Mr. Yu, a new teacher, was taking attendance and smiled just a little in Ruby's direction.

Ruby sat as straight as a chopstick at her desk. She had always wanted to be a teacher's pet, and she knew that teachers were easily impressed by good posture. Indeed, Mr. Yu called on Ruby next.

"Ruby Lu," Mr. Yu called, looking straight at Ruby.

Ruby sprang from her seat. "Present!" she cried, just as she had planned. She had decided that "present" would sound more third-grade than "here," which she had used since kindergarten.

A titter went through the class.

Ruby ignored it and sat down.

"Are you a polyglot?" Mr. Yu asked.

"Polly?" said Ruby. "I'm not Polly. I'm Ruby Lu."

Mr. Yu smiled. He turned and spelled P-O-L-Y-G-L-O-T on the board. "A polyglot is someone who speaks many languages," he explained. "Polyglots can be very useful in helping us understand different cultures."

The class was hushed. All eyes were on Ruby. This made Ruby sit as tall as a Seafair Queen going by on a parade float, and smile like one, too.

For a new teacher, Mr. Yu was okay. Ruby decided that she liked him. He seemed to know a lot. But he couldn't possibly know much about Ruby's school yet, so she decided that she would try to be as helpful as possible.

"My cousin Flying Duck is from China," said Ruby, pointing to Flying Duck, who was sitting next to her. "She's a polyglot too. She's deaf, so she can lip-read and use Chinese Sign Language, and she's learning American Sign Language."

Flying Duck smiled and saluted Mr. Yu with her right hand bouncing off her right eyebrow.

"That's 'hello' in Chinese Sign Language," Ruby said helpfully.

"Wow," said Mr. Yu.

"Yup," said Ruby. "And I'm going to be a third-grade teacher when I grow up."

"That's great," said Mr. Yu, smiling at Ruby and saluting Flying Duck back.

Ruby beamed. From the PTA newsletter that

Ruby's mom had read, Ruby knew that Mr. Yu was fresh out of teacher school. His hobbies included stamp collecting and trout fishing.

"One of the most exciting things about third grade is learning to become better communicators," said Mr. Yu. "Learning to speak a second language and being able to express yourself in different ways are very important."

Ruby sighed. She looked out the window. A cloud drifted by that looked like a dog. She thought about all the ways that she communicated with Elvis.

Then she sighed again.

She really missed being with her dog.

Ruby stared at the clock above the door. She counted the circles the long hand would have to make before she could walk through that door and go to dog obedience school. Six. Plus one more hour before obedience school started at four. Seven *long* hours.

Maybe Elvis was lonely, Ruby thought.

"One of the oldest ways of expressing ourselves is by writing haiku," said Mr. Yu.

Did he say hiking? Ruby didn't hear everything Mr. Yu was saying. Her teacher probably liked hiking, just like her dad, she thought. But Ruby didn't like hiking. It made her hungry and tired. But she did like show-and-tell. Hey, what happened to show-and-tell?

Ruby's hand shot up.

"Yes, Ruby?" said Mr. Yu, stopping in midsentence.

"Usually we do show-and-tell first," said Ruby helpfully. "I really don't want to do any hiking."

The class burst into laughter.

"We're doing haiku, not hiking," said Mr. Yu.

Oops.

"It's a very old form of Japanese poetry," Mr. Yu explained. "But you don't have to be Japanese or old to write it.

"We write haiku when it's hard to say how we're feeling," Mr. Yu continued. "A haiku shows what happened at the moment you had those feelings, so that your reader can have similar feelings of their own."

Then Mr. Yu wrote something on the board. He said it was a famous haiku.

> *Giant firefly:*
> *That way, this way, that way, this—*
> *And it passes by.*

Ruby liked fireflies. For a moment it felt like a warm summer night.

She raised her hand.

"Are we going to have show-and-tell?" she asked impatiently. "We always have show-and-tell."

Mr. Yu blinked. He looked at Ruby.

And Ruby looked slowly around. Something told her that show-and-tell was not part of the third-grade program.

"Ruby," said Mr. Yu, "would you like to help me write the haiku rules on the board?"

"Okay!" said Ruby, though she wasn't really okay without show-and-tell. But she did like writing on the board. "~~Hi koo~~ Haiku rules," she wrote. Then she wrote the rest just as Mr. Yu told it to her:

1. Write three lines.
2. Five syllables in the first line.
3. Seven syllables in the second line.
4. Five syllables in the third line.
5. Write about nature or anything you'd like.

Then Ruby marched back to her seat. From her desk, she admired the fancy loops and extra curlicues that she had added to the tops and bottoms of her letters to make them look like cursive. But no one else seemed to notice. Everyone else was bent like question marks over their haiku.

Ruby was the only one who was as straight as an exclamation point. She couldn't think of anything to write. All she could think of was Elvis.

Elvis was without Ruby for the first time.

He was home alone.

What if Elvis got sick?!!!

Ruby swallowed. Elvis could get very sick. He had a habit of eating socks and underwear. What if he choked?

Ruby raised her hand again.

"Yes?" said Mr. Yu.

"IT'S MY FIRST TIME AWAY FROM MY DOG," Ruby blurted. "AND TO BE PERFECTLY HONEST, I'M NOT FEELING THAT GREAT."

Heads lifted. Pencils stopped.

Mr. Yu blinked rapidly. His mouth opened, but nothing came out.

"ACTUALLY, I THINK I NEED TO GO HOME," Ruby said, climbing out of her desk and heading straight for the door.

"Wait," said Mr. Yu.

Ruby stopped. She clutched her chest. She took a deep breath.

"You're having the perfect haiku moment," Mr. Yu added. "Why don't you write about missing your dog?"

"Really?" asked Ruby.

Mr. Yu nodded.

"But what if he dies while I'm writing about him?" Ruby asked.

"Dies?" said Mr. Yu.

"He could be choking to death right this minute!" said Ruby. "I need to go home and make sure that he's okay."

Mr. Yu did a deep knee bend. He looked Ruby smack in the eye.

"I got my first dog when I was your age," he said. "I worried about him too, until I realized that he was

very smart. Dogs can take care of themselves. In fact, most of them are good at guarding your house, too."

Silence.

"I forgot," said Ruby. Her dad had said something about Elvis making a good guard dog.

So Ruby returned to her seat.

It was very quiet. Everyone was scratching away at their haiku. Everyone, that is, except Ruby. She stared at the tip of her pencil where words usually come out. But no words came out. She twisted one pigtail. Then she twisted the other. Still, no words came out.

Writing a haiku was like putting together a jigsaw puzzle, Ruby thought. Instead of a thousand little pieces, there were a million little feelings.

Worse, there were a million little words to describe those feelings.

Ruby swung her feet. Did Mr. Yu say something about counting syllables?

"What's a syllable?" Ruby whispered.

But it was too late.

"Who would like to read their haiku first?" asked Mr. Yu.

Christina's hand shot up. She had moved to Ruby's neighborhood from California. She wasn't like the rest of the children on Beacon Hill. She wore SPF 60 every day, and she knew all about the La Brea Tar Pits. She marched to the front of the room. She read:

> *"September morning*
> *I walk to school in new shoes*
> *Thoughts of toes in sand."*

Mr. Yu beamed. "Excellent, Christina!"
Ruby shrank.
Then Tiger's hand went up.
Tiger ran to the front of the room and waved his paper excitedly. Breathlessly he read:

> *"Fire trucks are red*
> *Screaming, roaring, rushing red*
> *Putting out fire's bed."*

"Fantastic, James!" said Mr. Yu, using Tiger's real name. "That's marvelous!"

"Thank you," said Tiger. "I like fire trucks."

"Me too," said Wally, who was Tiger's best friend. "But I like dinosaurs even more." So then Wally went next.

He stood next to the teacher's desk and read in his best dinosaur voice:

T. REX!

"T. rex, T. rex, T.
Roaring, slurping, drinking tea
Pinky up! T. rex!"

Ruby's heart pounded in her ears. She could tell that Mr. Yu was very impressed with all the haiku so far. He was saying something to Wally, who was smiling so widely his face looked like a balloon. Ruby wished that Wally would just float away like a balloon, then Mr. Yu would have to call 9-1-1 and forget all about making his class write haiku.

But Wally didn't float away. He sat down.

Then Mr. Yu looked for someone else to read.

Ruby held her breath.

"Ruby?" said Mr. Yu.

Ruby dragged her feet across the floor. Usually she loved reading in front of the class. It was one of her talents. That is, when she had something to read.

This time, her paper was blank.

Her mind was blank.

And she stared blankly straight ahead.

She stood on one foot.

Then she stood on the other.

Finally she blurted:

> *"MY DOG'S IN TROUBLE!*
> *SEVEN HOURS OF TORTURE!*
> *I'M HERE, HE IS THERE!"*

Silence.

"That was amazing!" said Mr. Yu, clapping loudly. "You did that on the spot!"

Then everyone else started clapping.

"Yeah," shouted Wally, "you didn't even write anything!"

"And you didn't even blink!" said Emma.

"You might be the next Haiku Heroine!" cried Thomas.

The next Haiku Heroine? Ruby could hardly believe her ears. It would be a dream come true. And it would be all because of her dog.

Ruby closed her eyes.

She took a deep breath.

Then Ruby felt herself fill with more love for him than ever before.

Now the best thing about third grade was everything. Ruby loved her new class, her new teacher, and most of all, her new dog, who was waiting for her to come home.

CHAPTER THREE
How to Survive Hard Times

When Ruby and Flying Duck finally got home, it looked like everyone was waiting to go to dog obedience school. This was no surprise to Ruby, as her family did everything together; they even went to the doctor's together whenever one of them was sick. It was one of the things Ruby loved most about her family—no one ever had to go anywhere scary alone. But she was surprised that her dad was there.

"Are you coming to dog obedience school too, Dad?" Ruby asked excitedly. It was very unusual for her dad to be home so early from work.

"No, Ruby," said her dad.

"Are you sick?" Ruby asked, worried. Her dad had come home early once with the flu. He was a good worker and generally didn't miss work or leave early unless it was an emergency.

"No, Honey Bee," he said. "I'm not sick, but thanks for your concern."

Ruby liked it when he called her Honey Bee. It made her feel special, and it was also Oscar's nickname for her—Bee, because he couldn't yet say Ruby. But she was puzzled. She knew that missing work was like skipping school—her dad could get seriously busted.

"Do you remember that I had an important meeting with my boss this morning?" Ruby's dad asked, putting a hand on her shoulder.

Ruby nodded. Her dad had said that she was a smart third grader when she remembered this at breakfast.

"Well, the meeting was to tell me that I lost my job today," said Ruby's dad.

"Oh," said Ruby quietly. She knew it wasn't good news. Her friend Ally's mom had lost her job, and it meant that they had to move far away. Wally's dad lost his job too, but Wally, who was generally very talkative, never talked about it, so Ruby didn't know anything about that.

"Will we have to move?" asked Ruby.

"I hope not," said her dad. "But I don't know. We'll have to wait and see. But there will certainly be some changes."

"What kind of changes?" asked Ruby.

"Well, Sweet Bee," Ruby's dad began, kneeling beside her. He looked Ruby smack in the eye. He took a deep breath.

"I know how much you've been looking forward to going to dog obedience school," said Ruby's dad, pulling her close. "But I'm afraid we won't be able to afford that now."

"Oh," said Ruby, very softly.

"I've got two weeks' pay, but after that, I won't

have another paycheck . . . for who knows how long," said her dad.

"None?" asked Ruby.

Ruby's father shook his head.

"What's going to happen to us?" Ruby asked, feeling scared. There were four grown-ups, three children, and one dog, and none of them had a job. Who was going to pay the bills? How were they going to heat their home? How were they going to buy food? As a third grader, Ruby could easily see that they were in trouble.

"Don't worry—," her dad began.

But Ruby interrupted, "Will we starve? What are we going to eat? How are you going to buy diapers for Oscar?

"And what about doctors' bills?" she continued. "And heating bills and car payments and house payments?"

Ruby's parents' eyes grew big and wide.

Ruby knew that her parents sometimes stayed up late talking about making payments and worrying about how much things cost. They lived on a budget, which Ruby understood was like her allowance. It meant that you couldn't buy all the candy you wanted, but you could have a special treat. Her parents were careful about what they bought. Her mom clipped coupons. They waited for things to go on sale. They shopped around for the lowest prices. And for very expensive things, like their car, they bought secondhand. But it never occurred to Ruby that her parents could run out of money altogether.

"Losing a job is hard on everyone," said Ruby's mom, putting an arm around Ruby and her dad. "Stretching our money further so that we'll have enough for what we really need isn't going to be easy," she said, "but the important thing is that we're going to do it together."

Ruby's dad hugged them both.

"I know this is very disappointing," Ruby's dad said to her. "But I don't want you to worry. That's my job."

Ruby looked at her parents. They looked like they were trying to be very brave. Her dad's eyes were wide open like when he was driving in the dark. And her mom looked a bit like she was about to get on a scary ride at the Fun Forest. Then Ruby watched her aunt and uncle give Flying Duck the news in sign language. The grown-ups all looked very worried.

"Will you find another job soon, Daddy?" Ruby asked.

"I hope so," said her dad.

"What if you don't?" asked Ruby. She wondered

if losing a job was like losing a shoe, which sometimes could take a long time to find, or worse, a sock, which often never reappeared.

"If that happens," said her dad, "I'll have to come up with a Plan B."

Ruby knew all about Plan Bs. Plan A was the regular way of doing things, and Plan B was when you used your imagination. She had come up with lots of Plan Bs herself, especially when it came to Oscar. Plan A might involve playing with Oscar. But if Ruby didn't want to play with him, she could set him in front of the TV (Plan B). B stood for better, just like it did on her report cards.

But Ruby didn't feel any better.

The little hand on the kitchen clock was now pointing to the four.

Ruby had waited a long time for this hour.

She closed her eyes. She could almost hear a roomful of dogs barking. . . .

And smell their doggie breaths . . .

And feel their wagging tails hitting her legs . . .

Ruby blinked.

The only tail hitting her was Elvis's. He had a tennis ball balanced on the top of his head. He was so silly. He winked at her. Then he smiled. His tongue came out. It flapped like a little piece of laundry in the wind.

Ruby blinked back tears. It was four o'clock, and dog obedience school was starting without them.

"Elvis says it's okay, Dad," Ruby said bravely. "He didn't want to go anyway."

But Ruby did. She wanted to go to dog obedience school real bad. Her friend Emma had gone with her dog, Elwyn. And Elwyn was the best-behaved dog on 20th Avenue South. And Ruby wanted Elvis to behave like that too.

It wasn't fair.

Ruby's lips quivered.

A tear rolled down one cheek.

Another tear rolled down the other.

Then Ruby fell on Elvis and hugged him and cried full blast.

Her dad was right. She was very disappointed.

And whenever Ruby cried, so did Oscar.

And whenever Oscar cried, so did Flying Duck.

And when all the children were cry-ing at Ruby's house, you could hear it all the way down the street.

The best thing about crying your eyes out on 20th Avenue South was that everyone would come running.

Emma, who lived next door to Ruby, was the first one to climb into the branches of the plum tree in Ruby's backyard. Then Tiger and Wally rushed over. And Christina came

running from across the street. Then Panchito, the new Mexican kid, who was always too shy to come over until now.

It was an emergency meeting of the 20th Avenue Plum Club. The Plum Club met whenever there was anything to do or for no reason at all. Ruby was the president because the plum tree was in her backyard, and everyone else was a member. Mostly the club met in the summertime when there was nothing to do. But it also met whenever there was a ruckus in the neighborhood.

And after Ruby told them the bad news, it got very quiet in the plum tree.

At first no one knew what to say. But everyone knew Ruby's family was in for some hard times.

"You're going to be poor," said Tiger.

"You'll get food stamps," said Wally.

"The bank will take away your house," said Christina. "You could end up living in a cardboard box under the freeway."

Ruby sucked in her breath. It was worse than she had imagined.

"You won't have any friends," added Panchito, who didn't have any friends. He had always kept to himself. In fact, everyone was surprised that he had suddenly joined the Plum Club.

"What are you going to do?" Wally asked.

"Dunno," said Ruby. "I'm just a kid."

"My dad says you need to be in the right place at the right time to get any kind of job these days," said Emma.

"How do you do that?" asked Ruby.

"Dunno," said Emma.

No one knew. It was a complete mystery.

But the best thing about emergency meetings was that you got lots of good advice for free. And Ruby's friends knew a lot of things. Everyone had something to say, and Ruby wrote it all down just as her friends told it to her:

How to Survive Hard Times

1. Go to the library.
2. Check out books on dog training.
3. Do it yourself.
4. Start a business.
5. Sell something!
6. Make some money.
7. Scan some twenty-dollar bills.
8. Cut carefully.
9. Think positively.
10. Look alive.
11. Keep your head up.
12. Eat chocolate cake.
13. Listen to happy music.

Ruby looked at her list. There was a lot to do. In fact, her mom would probably call it daunting, which meant you better get off your butt or else!

CHAPTER FOUR
Job Search Central

Surviving hard times was not at all what Ruby had expected.

First, everyone at school was very sympathetic. All Ruby had to do was mention that her father had lost his job, and she got all sorts of special attention.

"Ruby," said Mr. Yu, "would you like the job of being our class attendance person? You'd have to take our attendance sheet and lunch order to the main office every day."

Ruby could hardly believe it. It was a special job for a special student, and she got it, just like that.

Then in music class, Miss Esteban asked if Ruby would like the job of passing out the recorders. Ruby was speechless. She had waited all her life to play the recorder in third grade, but she never imagined that she'd also be passing them out!

Then, in haiku practice, Ruby got the job of reaching into the jar and pulling out the topic of the day:

My favorite pet

It was perfect! Ruby didn't write just one haiku about Elvis, she wrote several. Then she picked her best one and read it aloud to the class. It went like this:

Ruby Lu

Elvis is my dog:
He clowns, juggles, and cycles
One cool, furry dude!

But that was not all.

During library hour, the librarian read a story to the class about a brave little girl named Ruby who went to school where no one wanted her because she was black. Every day she walked through howling crowds to learn her lessons from a teacher in an empty classroom in an empty building because all the parents had pulled their children out.

"If you get afraid," the other Ruby's mom told her daughter, "say your prayers. You can pray to God anytime, anywhere. He will always hear you."

The other Ruby's bravery helped make it possible for kids of all races to go to school together.

It was a true story.

Ruby loved it. She imagined that she was brave like that too.

And she was.

Every day she began marching to school with her head held high, just like the other Ruby. There were no angry mobs shouting at her, but she often enjoyed pretending to be the people she read about in books.

But the best part about surviving hard times was after school.

When Ruby and Flying Duck got home in the afternoons, it was Job Search Central around the kitchen table. Ruby's mom and dad took turns reading want ads, checking for jobs online, sending e-mails, and calling people on the phone. There were coffee cups, seaweed crackers, and cookies everywhere. It was like a regular party!

Ruby jumped right in to help. Her mom showed her how to read the want ads and circle any that she thought were interesting.

Soon Ruby was doing more than reading and circling the ads. She searched the internet. She checked websites. One day, she even sent an e-mail and attached her dad's résumé. "Hello," Ruby typed in her e-mail. "I'm looking 4 a job 4 my dad. Here's his resumay. He's a good werker. He was born that way. He goes to werk every day except Saturdays and Sundays. He's a grate dad 2. Please give him a job. And please write back. Sincerely, Ruby Lu."

But no one wrote back.

Fortunately, Ruby's mom had better luck.

"I got a job!" cried Ruby's mom, after getting off the phone one afternoon.

"That's fantastic!" said Ruby's dad. "Congratulations!"

"They're hiring me to sell shoes in the mall," Ruby's mom explained. "I'll only be making minimum wage, but I'll get a commission for every pair I sell, and it'll all add up."

Ruby's dad gave her mom a hug and a kiss.

Flying Duck's parents congratulated Ruby's mom on her good luck.

And Flying Duck thumped her chest and gave her aunt a salute.

But Ruby did not. She stopped completely in her tracks.

"The job is for *you*?" she peeped. The words fell off her tongue like sour tofu.

"Of course," said Ruby's mom.

"I thought it was for *Dad*," said Ruby. "I thought we were helping *Dad* find a job."

It had never occurred to Ruby that her mom was looking for a job for herself. Her mom already had a job as a volunteer in the school library.

"Who's going to be home after school?" Ruby squawked.

"Your dad will be here," said her mom.

"What if Oscar runs into a tree?"

"What if Flying Duck needs a translation?"

"What if the house burns down?"

"Rubee . . . ," said Ruby's mom.

Ruby didn't like the idea of her mom going to work at all. Everything at home depended on her mom being there. Didn't her mom realize that she was the sun and everyone else was cosmic dust? If the sun got up and walked off to another job, wouldn't the entire universe freeze to death?

"What if I have a bad day at school?" Ruby continued.

"What if I get food poisoning?"

"What if I die?"

Ruby breathed in. Then she breathed out. She didn't feel so good.

"What if I don't love you anymore?" Ruby asked spitefully. A tear rolled down her cheek.

"I will still love you, Ruby Lu," said Ruby's mom, putting her arms around Ruby and pulling her close.

Ruby's mother held her for a long time. She smoothed her hair. She wiped her tears.

"I will *always* love you," Ruby's mother whispered, squeezing her tight. "Change is hard on everyone. But my love for you will never change."

CHAPTER FIVE
The Good News, the Bad News

Ruby's mom went to work, just like that.

And Ruby's dad stayed home.

At school, Ruby overheard a conversation on the playground. It went like this:

Boy hanging upside down: "Did you hear? Ruby's dad lost his job."

Boy lying underneath on the wood chips: "Yup."

Upside-down boy: "Dads who don't have jobs are losers."

Right-side-up boy: "Yup. I'd sure hate to have a loser dad."

Upside-down boy: "Chump. Me too."

Ruby blinked. Was her dad a loser? She didn't

know. So every day after school, Ruby kept a careful
eye on her dad. And this is what she saw:

He drank a lot of coffee.

He ate a lot of cookies.

He changed a lot of diapers.

He waited around the phone a lot.

He was boring.

When he wasn't being boring, he would try to
be useful.

He took everyone to the library.

He learned a little sign language (from a library
book and from Flying Duck).

He let the dog out.

He boiled things. Pacifiers. Toys. Jewelry. Anything that mysteriously fell into the toilet.

He boiled other things too. Spaghetti. Eggs. Water.

But he didn't know how to use the rice cooker. So it was a good thing Ruby and Flying Duck did!

He couldn't figure out how much detergent to use in the washing machine.

And when it came to giving cute little Oscar, who was as slippery as a sea lion, a bath, Ruby's dad made a complete mess.

Ruby's dad wasn't a loser, but he was definitely not the center of the universe like Ruby's mom. He wasn't even the captain of the ship.

But still, he was Ruby's dad, and she found many things that she liked about having him at home.

First, Ruby liked the job applications. Her dad always picked up a few extras, just in case. This meant that Ruby and Flying Duck could fill them out and pretend that they were looking for jobs too.

Second, Ruby liked the way her dad vacuumed. Instead of vacuuming around everything, he lifted the furniture like a superhero and vacuumed

underneath it. He even lifted Ruby, Oscar, and Flying Duck, if they happened to be on the furniture. Oscar liked that a lot.

"Again!" Oscar shouted. "Again!"

Third, Ruby liked the way he did the laundry. It was not the same way that her mom did laundry. When Ruby's mom did laundry, everything always came back the same, except clean. When Ruby's dad did laundry, you never knew how something would come back. It was a complete surprise. It could be too small, too big, suddenly pink, or totally unrecognizable! It was like having a whole new wardrobe.

Fourth, Ruby liked the card games. Her dad was a Scrabble maniac, but he was also a card shark. This meant that he was very smart at playing all of Ruby's favorites like Old Maid, Egyptian Rat Screw, and War. He also taught Ruby and Flying Duck how to play many new games, such as poker, rummy, and bridge.

But that was not all.

Ruby's dad was a big help when it came to dog training. Ruby and Flying Duck had checked out all sorts of dog training books and videos at the library, including:

How to Make Your Dog Mind Without Losing Yours.
Train Your Dog Before He Trains You.
Improve Your Life, Train Your Dog.

Ruby and Flying Duck read the books and watched the videos over and over again. But they still couldn't get it right.

"Heel, boy," said Ruby, looking at the photographs in a book.

Elvis jumped on Ruby.

"Down!" Flying Duck commanded in sign language.

Elvis got down all right . . . and jumped on Flying Duck.

But when Ruby's dad read the instructions to Ruby, something happened.

"An obedient dog is a happy dog," read Ruby's dad. "If you want to train your dog, you must take charge and let him know he has a leader to follow."

Ruby tried again.

"Sit," she said in her best dog-commanding voice.

Elvis sat.

Ruby could hardly believe it! So her dad read some more.

"Dogs want to obey," her dad continued. "They are pack animals. Your family is their pack. And every pack needs a leader—an alpha dog."

Ruby's head tilted with the thought. She liked the idea of being a pack of dogs.

"Dogs feel insecure without an alpha dog," read Ruby's dad. "If *you* are not that alpha dog, your dog will act up and become the leader."

"Shake," Ruby commanded, extending her hand.

Elvis shook.

"Dad! I'm an alpha dog!" Ruby cried.

Her dad laughed. "That you are," he said.

But when Ruby read the instructions without her dad, Elvis ignored her again.

So Ruby knew who the *real* alpha dog was. It was her dad, and she felt very proud of him.

But best of all, Ruby liked just being with her alpha dad.

"Dad," Ruby said while they were sitting together on the couch one afternoon.

"Mmm," said Ruby's dad.

"If I wanted to start a business, what could I do?" asked Ruby.

"Well, you could do anything," said her dad. "First you'd have to decide if you want to sell a product or a service."

"What's the difference?" asked Ruby.

"Do you want to sell stuff, or do you want to sell something useful that you do—like walking dogs or raking leaves?" asked Ruby's dad.

"I don't know," said Ruby.

"Well, selling a service is a good idea because you don't need much, if any, money to get started," her dad advised her. "All you need is to roll up your sleeves."

"Roll up your sleeves?" asked Ruby, puzzled.

Ruby's dad chuckled. "That's an expression,"

he said. "It means a willingness to work."

Ruby smiled. She loved talking to her dad. He knew a lot of things, especially strange expressions like that. And it was easy for her to talk to him, because he was sitting around watching TV *all* the time now. So Ruby, Flying Duck, and Oscar watched *a lot* of TV too, unlike when Ruby's mom used to be home and they never had any time for TV, or for talking on the couch.

"Could you make more popcorn, Dad?" Ruby asked.

"Pop!" said Oscar eagerly. "Pop, pop!"

"Sure!" said Ruby's dad, going to the kitchen. "Great idea."

"Dad," Ruby called out, "could you stay home all the time?"

"I *am* at home all the time," said her dad.

"I mean never go back to work," said Ruby, throwing her arms around her dad when he came back with their snack. "I like having you around."

"Thanks, Ruby," said her dad. "I like having you around too."

Surviving hard times was nothing like what Ruby had expected. In fact, it didn't feel like hard times at all.

Until . . .

Ruby's report card came home.

Usually, Ruby's report card showed that she was generally paying attention and was doing A work, and mostly B work for better! But this time there weren't any As . . . or Bs . . . or even Cs . . . but there sure were a lot of Ds.

"Oh dear," said Ruby's mom, who hadn't been home to supervise homework.

"D is for Didn't Fail," said Ruby hopefully, but she had a bad, sinking feeling that she hadn't gotten it precisely right.

"Ruby," said her mom, "have you been having trouble with your homework?"

"Homework?" asked Ruby "What homework?"

"Yeah, what homework?" echoed Ruby's dad. "Third graders don't get homework."

Silence.

"Do they?"

Later that night, after Ruby and Flying Duck and Oscar had gone to bed, but the girls were not yet asleep, Ruby heard her mom and dad have an argument for the first time since her dad lost his job.

"This place looks like a circus!" said Ruby's mom. She sounded worried about many things.

And Ruby's father sounded worried too.

For a long time Ruby listened to the sound of grown-up voices drifting up into her room. Usually she liked the sound of grown-up voices coming from the kitchen. It was a lullaby at night, and in the mornings, it was an alarm clock. It meant the end of a day or the beginning of another. It was the sound of everything that was right.

But now, nothing was right.

"I wish I could do something to help my mom and dad," Ruby whispered into her moonlit room.

"Urrrrr," said Elvis, who was falling asleep at the foot of Ruby's bed.

"Oh, Elvis," said Ruby, wrapping her arms around her dog. "What's going to happen to us?"

"Mmmm," said Elvis. "Mmmmm."

Ruby could see his dark, wet eyes looking sadly at her through the denim-colored night. He was giving her all sorts of advice. And she listened with all her heart.

Elvis told Ruby a lot of things.

He had lived another life.

He knew about surviving hard times.

"That's it!" said Ruby. She clicked on her flashlight and popped out of bed. In the top drawer of her desk was a long-forgotten list, "How to Survive Hard Times."

"I'd forgotten all about this," said Ruby, slipping back into her warm bed.

Then by flashlight the two of them looked over the list together.

"I'm going to start this tomorrow," said Ruby with as much determination as she could muster after a long day.

"Urrrrr?" said Elvis.

"I love you, Elvis," said Ruby sleepily.

"Wuuuuv." Elvis exhaled, covering Ruby's little feet with his chin.

Then they slipped into their dreams.

REP[ORT C]ARD
Mr. Yu
ENGL[ISH]
HISTORY   D
GYM   D
SPANISH

CHAPTER SIX
Sneaky, Send Notes Home with Grades

No one said much at breakfast the next day. No one knew what to say. Ruby's dad was still in his robe and was glum and silent. Ruby's mom looked tired and sad and was dressed in a dark suit and had on her Sunday shoes for her job at the mall.

"I need a spa," said Ruby's mom. "I need a massage, I need a haircut, I need to just get off my feet."

Clak-clak-clak! went her mom's shoes across the kitchen floor. *Clak-clak-clak!* Her shoes came back the other way. Ruby thought about the time she'd gone to a spa with her mom. Her mom had been in a good mood then, not like the crabby mood that she was often in after work or that she was in now.

Sluuurp! went Ruby's cereal. *Slurp-SLUUUURP!*

"Ruby, please remember your manners," Ruby's dad said abruptly.

"And remember to hand in your report card," Ruby's mom reminded her. "I also put a note in there for your teacher."

"A note?" asked Ruby.

"It's a reply to his note," said her mom. "Your teacher suggested that you stay after school for some tutoring until your grades improve, and I agreed."

Silence.

"What's tutoring?" asked Ruby.

"Mr. Yu's going to help you study," said her mom.

"But Dad can help me," said Ruby.

"I'm sorry, Ruby," said Ruby's dad. "But I've got to really focus on my job search now. If you need help with your homework after tutoring, I'll be here for that."

"But I have plans after school," Ruby protested. "I wanted to join some clubs and then hang out with Elvis and Flying Duck."

"Honey," said Ruby's mom, "when your grades improve, you can make other plans."

"But it's important," said Ruby, letting her spoon clink loudly in her bowl.

Ruby's mom gave her a look. "Your grades are important, young lady," she said firmly.

Ruby felt terrible. Not only had she upset her dad, but now she'd upset her mom. It was not a good sign.

So Ruby closed her eyes and said her prayers all the way up 20th Avenue South and down the street to school.

By the time attendance was taken, the entire third-grade class knew all about Ruby's dismal report card.

By the time it was morning recess, Ruby's prayers for Mr. Yu had not been answered. He had not yet been swallowed by a big fish.

Normally, Mr. Yu was okay. Ruby liked him fine. But this was not normal. Was a report card with all Ds *normal*? Was sending a note home that

Ruby didn't see *normal*? Was ruining all of Ruby's afternoons *normal*? The more Ruby thought about this, the angrier she became. So she decided that she didn't like Mr. Yu very much at all anymore.

During art class, she drew a picture of Mr. Yu trout fishing.

First came the mosquitoes.

Then came the sunburn.

Then came the shark. *Snap! Snap!*

"Help me!" Mr. Yu cried in the picture. "I should have been nicer to Ruby!"

Ruby thought she would feel better, but she didn't.

She felt terrible.

"Ruby," said Mr. Yu during math class, "what is Flying Duck trying to tell me?"

Ruby looked at Flying Duck, who was signing that she needed help.

"She says that math story problems are her favorite," said Ruby.

"Great!" said Mr. Yu, giving Flying Duck a thumbs-up.

Ruby knew that her cousin could not do math story problems.

But Ruby wasn't about to be helpful to a mean old teacher who was ruining her life, was she?

Then, in haiku practice, the topic that came out of the jar was "monsters."

When it was Ruby's turn, she boldly read what she had written:

> *"Monsters are creepy*
> *Sneaky, send notes home with grades.*
> *Monsters should not teach."*

Everyone gasped.

Ruby marched back to her seat. She sat down.

She thought the angry haiku would make her feel better, but it didn't.

She felt even worse than when she was praying for the big fish.

And worse than when she drew the mean picture.

In fact, Ruby felt so bad, she couldn't hold it in any longer.

"I'm not going to be a third-grade teacher when I grow up," she said. "I'm going to be the principal."

Silence.

Time-out.

"Ruby," said Mr. Yu, "may I speak with you in private?"

Ruby shrank. She was really busted now.

All eyes followed her.

"Ruby," said Mr. Yu in the hallway, lowering his voice to a whisper, "I know you're mad at me."

Ruby looked at the floor.

"And I know you're going through a lot right now," said Mr. Yu. "But I hope that you'll give me a chance to help you do better work in school."

Ruby looked at the ceiling.

She stood on one foot.

Then she stood on the other.

What a horrible day she was having! The bad mood at breakfast had followed her to school and gotten worse and worse. Ruby wished she could put the day in reverse and start over again.

"I'll tell you what," said Mr. Yu. "If you're not ready for tutoring today, we can start tomorrow."

Ruby stood on both feet.

Really? She could hardly believe her ears.

"Tomorrow?" she asked.

"Sometimes we just need more time to warm up to a new idea," said Mr. Yu. "You can come today, or you can wait until tomorrow. You decide."

Ruby's head tilted with this thought.

She liked it.

She liked the idea of deciding something for herself.

"Okay," she said finally.

Then, for the first time all day, Ruby felt much better.

CHAPTER SEVEN
Open for Business

Now that it was her decision, Ruby wanted to go to tutoring almost as much as she had wanted to go to dog obedience school. But of course, she needed to wait a day, just so Mr. Yu would know who was in charge.

So she rushed home with Flying Duck.

It was a good thing she did, because there was an emergency meeting of the 20th Avenue Plum Club. They didn't even have time to go into the house, they climbed right into the tree.

"You can't go to tutoring," warned Christina, from a branch above Ruby. She had overheard Ruby's hallway conversation with their teacher. In fact, they had all heard it. Whenever anyone got busted in the hallway, the whole class would hear everything.

"Why not?" asked Ruby.

"Because it costs money," said Christina. "That's how teachers make extra money. And if your dad doesn't have a job, how are you going to pay for it?"

"My mom didn't say anything about that," said Ruby.

"Maybe she didn't want you to worry," said Wally, hanging upside down from his branch.

Didn't want her to worry? Could Wally be right? Her mom and dad didn't discuss their money troubles with her. She didn't know if they had any money in the bank . . . or if they were rich or poor. In fact, before Ruby's dad lost his job, she really didn't think about money beyond her weekly allowance, which she always spent on candy at Fred's.

But Ruby did notice that her parents had become very careful about spending, even more than usual. They bought rice, but they didn't buy cakes and pies from the bakery anymore. They wrote e-mails, but they didn't make phone calls to China. They watched TV, but they no longer went to the movies. They quit bowling on Friday nights and stayed home to play mah-jongg, which was also a lot of exercise. And last week, instead of going to the barbershop, Ruby's dad sat in the kitchen and got his hair cut by Ruby's mom. Ruby had never seen them do that before.

"How much money?" Ruby asked.

"Three hundred bucks," said Christina.

"That's a lot of money," said Ruby.

"It's a lot of dough," Christina said. "In California, only the rich kids get tutored."

"Oh," said Ruby, hanging on to her branch a little tighter.

Ruby liked to imagine that she and her friends were little birds in her tree. But today she felt like a bowling pin, and the bowling ball of disappointment had just knocked her over.

"Well, heck, I would help you if I had the money," said Tiger.

"Me too," said Emma.

"Not me," said Panchito. "I wouldn't help you."

"Why not?" asked Wally.

"*No me gusto,*" said Panchito.

"You *no me gusto* every-thing," said Christina.

Christina was right. Panchito was very annoy-ing in that way. He didn't like anything or anybody. He didn't even like candy.

"Then you can just go home," said Emma.

"No," said Panchito. "I want to stay."

"Then get with the program," said Christina, who could be kind of bossy.

"*No quiero hacerlo,*" said Panchito.

"Fine," said Emma. "Then we're just going to ignore you."

"Fine," said Panchito.

And that was the end of that. It was the same way with Panchito at recess. He never went along with the program, and everyone just ignored him.

Ruby's friends were right. Her parents couldn't afford to pay Mr. Yu for tutoring, at least not until her dad found a job again . . . or . . . if she somehow came up with the money herself.

That was it!

"I'm going to pay for it myself," said Ruby.

"How?" asked Emma.

Ruby pulled out "How to Survive Hard Times" from her pocket. "I'm going to start my own business," she said. "And you can all be my customers."

"Hooray!" said Wally, shaking the tree so that the leaves were applauding.

"I'll be your first customer!" cried Tiger.

"Me too!" signed Flying Duck.

"But none of us has any money," said Christina.

"No problem," said Ruby, reading her sheet of survival tips. "Make some money. Scan some twenty-dollar bills. Cut carefully."

No one had a twenty-dollar bill, but Emma had a five-dollar bill left over from her birthday money.

Flying Duck had a crisp twenty renminbi note from China. And eventually Christina coughed up a ten-dollar bill.

Then Ruby's friends all ran next door to Emma's house, where there was a color copy machine and scanner in her mom's office.

By the time they had carefully cut out all their bills and stuffed their wallets full and run back to Ruby's backyard, Ruby was ready and waiting. Her tent was open for business. The sign she hung out in her best cursive handwriting said:

Ruby's Plum Tree Spa

Underneath it was a menu:

HAIRCUT: $10

FACIAL: $10

NAILS: $10

RELAXATION: $10

PUT UP YOUR FEET: Free

THE WORKS: $40

And the fine print at the bottom said:

If you're my mom: Free

"Wow," said Christina. Her mouth dropped open.

Flying Duck whistled. She gave Ruby two thumbs-up.

"Bring it on!" said Emma. "I've never been to a real spa before."

"I don't like spas," said Panchito.

"You don't like anything," said Ruby.

"It's just for girls," said Panchito.

Ruby's Plum Tree Spa
Haircut $10
Facial $10
nails $10
Relaxation $10
Put up your feet free
The Works $40

"Embrace your inner girl," said Ruby. "Dudes go to spas. I've seen them there."

"Ruby's been to a real spa with her mom," said Emma.

"Yup," said Ruby. "You come out a new person. It's called a makeover."

"*Owwwoooo!*" Elvis howled approvingly.

"Gimme the works," said Tiger.

"Me too," said Wally.

So Ruby gave them the works.

Snip, snip.

Clip, clip.

Spackle, spackle. (The clay mask needed to be put on thick.)

Sip, sip. (She served a refreshing lemonade.)

Polish, polish.

"More!" said Tiger.

"More!" said Emma, fanning herself.

"More??" asked Ruby. Playing spa was more fun than she could have imagined. She loved snipping and clipping and polishing!

So Ruby gave them more of everything.

Even Elvis got in on some of the action. *"Owwwwooo!"* he howled approvingly when Ruby combed his fur. Then he paid her in kisses.

Only Panchito stood watching, because he said he wasn't the least bit interested, but you could tell that he was *this* close to jumping right in. And Oscar watched too, from the window. He was stuck inside the house because Ruby's dad was on the phone.

By the time Ruby was done, her friends looked very relaxed and happy . . . and, well, changed.

And Ruby herself was quite changed too.

She now had enough money to pay Mr. Yu for tutoring so that her parents wouldn't have to.

Best of all, Ruby could hardly wait to see her mom's face when she saw a spa right in her own backyard.

CHAPTER EIGHT
The Phone Started Ringing Like Crazy

"How was tutoring today?" asked Ruby's dad when Ruby and Flying Duck finally came in from playing spa.

"Mr. Yu said I could start tomorrow," said Ruby. Her dad was behind his newspaper at the kitchen table. There were red circles all over the want ads. It meant that he had been very busy.

"That's wonderful," mumbled Ruby's dad, not once looking up from his newspaper. "I knew you'd like it."

"Did you find a job today, Dad?" asked Ruby.

Silence.

Oops. Ruby had a feeling that her dad didn't like being asked if he had found a job every day. But she couldn't help it. She'd forget, and the question would slip out of her mouth, just like that. In fact, it was the first question she always asked after school.

"I rolled up my sleeves and earned lots of money this afternoon," said Ruby proudly.

"That's nice, Honey Bee," said Ruby's dad, still behind the paper.

"That way you and mom won't have to worry about paying Mr. Yu for my tutoring," said Ruby.

Silence.

Ruby hated it when her dad was too busy to put down his paper. It was something her mom never did. So Ruby imagined having X-ray vision so that she could see her dad through the newspaper. She saw him secretly eating a gigantic stash of candy that he didn't want to share. This made Ruby giggle.

"What's so funny?" came Ruby's dad's voice.

"Nothing," said Ruby.

Silence.

"Good," said Ruby's dad. "Now . . . run along and do your homework. . . . I'll start dinner soon."

Ruby and Flying Duck ran along. And they made it as far as the living room, where Oscar and Elvis were watching TV, and they all cuddled up on the couch to watch cartoons . . . until . . .

The phone started ringing like crazy.

"What?" Ruby heard her dad say on the phone in the kitchen. *Blahblahblahblahblah.*  *Click.*

Riiiing, riiiing!

"That's not possible," he said. *Blahblahblahblahblah. Click.*

Riiiing, riiiing!

"Are you sure?" he asked. *Blahblahblahblahblah. Click.*

Riiing, riiiing!

"But Ruby was at tutoring this afternoon," he said. *Blahblahblahblahblah. Click.*

Riiiing, riiiing!

"But Ruby just got home," he said. *Blahblahblah-blahblah. Click.*

Long silence.

"RUBEEEE!" yelled Ruby's dad.

Ruby was SO busted.

It wasn't the clayey faces.

It wasn't the packing peanuts between the toes.

It wasn't even the black and blue and purple nail polish (on the boys). The girls got Scorching Pink.

It was the haircuts.

The very *bad* haircuts.

The *five* very bad haircuts.

And the four very angry parents, who brought their children over for Ruby's dad to see.

"What's going on?" asked Ruby's mom, when she came home from work.

"Aiyaaaah!" gasped Second Aunt as soon as she saw Flying Duck.

"Ruby," said Ruby's dad. "What were you doing?"

"They came to my spa," said Ruby. "And like you said, I just rolled up my sleeves."

"You did what?" asked Ruby's dad.

"I sold a useful service," said Ruby, "and they paid for it."

Her dad's eyes grew big and round.

"*Paid* for it?" he asked.

Ruby nodded. She pulled out her wad.

Ruby's dad's tongue fell out.

He fingered the money very carefully. He looked at the front of it, then he turned it over. Then he held it up to the light. But he was unable to speak.

"It's to pay for tutoring," said Christina.

"You should be proud of Ruby," said Wally.

"Ruby *worked* for it the *old-fashioned* way," said Tiger. "We made sure of it."

Ruby's dad put his head in his hands. He looked like he was about to cry.

"Don't worry, Mr. Lu," said Emma. "If we didn't pay Ruby enough, we can make more."

CHAPTER NINE
Pet Therapy

This is what you do when you're as busted as Ruby:

Eat your vegetables.
Eat *all* your vegetables.
Brush your teeth.
Floss.
Don't watch TV.
Do your homework.
Do *all* your homework.
Clean your room.
Train your dog.
Be nice to Oscar.
Go to tutoring.
Repeat.

This is called keeping a low profile. It was another one of Ruby's dad's strange sayings. It means to stay out of sight until everyone's forgotten about you and your criminal history.

Fog as thick as soup covered 20th Avenue South in the mornings now. Ruby wore lots of reflective tape, and she covered Flying Duck's coat in reflective tape too to keep her cousin safe. The air had gradually lost its summery blanket, and Ruby's family dressed in layers at home to keep warm. It wasn't wintry cold yet, but the weather had definitely changed. Often it rained a quiet, misty rain. And when it rained, the smell of sweet, rotten plums surrounded Ruby's house, and the grass underneath the tree in her back-yard became slick with the dark bodies of fallen and broken fruit.

Although Ruby no longer had to worry about paying for tutoring (because it was free), she wondered how they were going to make it through all the holidays that she loved. She had been especially looking forward to introducing Flying Duck to her favorite celebrations, but now Ruby wasn't so sure.

They were eating watery soup every night and a lot of plain white rice with a few vegetables left over from their summer garden.

How were they going to buy enough candy for Halloween? What would she do for a costume? Would they get a turkey for Thanksgiving? Would there be gravy and stuffing and sweet potato pie and Peking duck and vegetable dumplings and sushi? Would there be presents for Christmas? Would they get a tree? Would her parents take her shopping?

During haiku practice, when the subject was "my favorite holiday," Ruby wrote about her worries:

Halloween's for sweets,
Thanksgiving and Christmas—treats,
An old memory.

When Mr. Yu called on Ruby to read, she couldn't. She felt too sad. She couldn't even get up out of her seat.

Worse, everyone at school was buzzing about

Halloween. Every year there was a parade during lunch, and prizes were given for the best costumes. Moms and dads and grandparents came to take pictures, and everyone appeared on the school website, even pets and baby brothers. Ruby had brought home notices about the event and attached them with magnets to the refrigerator where all school notices go, but her parents had said nothing about them. Families were expected to bring snacks for a party after the parade, and normally her mom would be making plans for cupcakes or some other goody to bring to school, and she would be nearly finished with making Ruby's and Oscar's costumes by now, but this year things were not normal.

Ruby's mom was exhausted in the evenings and often crabby, just like her dad used to be after a rough day at work.

And Ruby's dad had changed like the weather.

The longer Ruby's dad was out of a job, the more boring he seemed to get. Instead of hiding behind his newspaper, he was now spending a lot of time in the bathroom.

And when he wasn't in the bathroom, he was in front of the TV.

He ate all the cookies.

He ate all the chips.

He drank all the coffee.

He did not shave.

He did not change his clothes.

He stopped doing laundry.

He stopped vacuuming.

And he stopped making red circles in the news-paper.

In other words, Ruby could see that her dad was in no mood to bake and sew for Halloween. But if they let Halloween go to the dogs, which was another one of her dad's strange expressions, the rest of the holidays were sure to follow.

So there was an emergency meeting of the 20th Avenue Plum Club during morning recess, right there on the school playground, without the plum tree.

"Sounds like your dad's in a funk," said Wally, "just like my dad." It was the first time Wally said anything about his dad since his dad lost his job a long time ago.

"Your dads need therapy," said Christina matter-of-factly, hopping and turning on one foot in the hopscotch squares.

"What's therapy?" asked Ruby.

"You pay someone lots of money to listen to you," said Christina. "And then you feel better!"

"How much money?" asked Ruby.

"Three hundred dollars," said Christina.

Wally whistled. "If my dad had three hundred dollars," he said, "he wouldn't need therapy."

"In that case, he can get *free* therapy," said Christina.

"Free therapy?" asked Ruby.

"You don't need any money," Christina explained. "You just need a pet."

"I've heard of that," said Emma. "It's called pet therapy. People's moods improve when they're petting an animal. It works with my dog, Elwyn.

"Just let Elvis do it," she added.

"Elvis?" asked Ruby.

"My mom says dog therapists come into the

hospital all the time," said Christina, whose mom was a nurse. "They make rounds just like the doctors."

Ruby wondered if Elvis would make a good therapist. He wasn't a normal dog. He had a mind and life of his own. But still, he was a good listener. Whenever Ruby needed someone to talk to, Elvis was there. And she always felt better after talking to him.

Pet therapy. Maybe it would work.

"Okay," said Ruby. "I'll give it a try."

So after school, Ruby hurried home.

She talked to Elvis.

Then she talked to Elvis some more.

First he balanced a ball on his nose.

Then he twirled on his hind feet.

Then he went over and sniffed Ruby's bike.

He was playing hard to get.

"Okay," said Ruby finally. "You can ride my bike if you help my dad."

Elvis made Ruby shake on it.

Then he followed her into the house.

"Hi, Dad!" said Ruby. "Did you find a job today?"

"Grrrrr," said her dad.

Oops.

Ruby had forgotten again. Her dad was on the couch watching TV. The paper with the classified ads was on the floor in front of him, and there were no red circles anywhere. It was not a good sign.

"Do you mind if Elvis watches TV with you?" Ruby asked.

"Grrrrr," said Ruby's dad.

Ruby put her dog next to her dad on the couch.

"Grrrrr," said Ruby's dad.

"Grrrrr," said Ruby's dog.

"Rrrrrr," said Ruby's dad.

"Rrrrrr," said Ruby's dog.

Then they watched TV together.

Neither of them said anything for a long, long time. The light in the room faded until their faces were lit only by the glow from the TV screen.

Finally Ruby's dad put his hand on Ruby's dog. He rubbed him between the ears.

Ruby's dog smiled.

His dog fur stood up.

"*Urrrrrrr,*" he purred. "*Urrrrrrr.*" He was as cute as he could be.

So Ruby's dad rubbed him some more.

"Silly dog," said Ruby's dad.

Then he smiled.

It was the first time Ruby had seen him smile in a long time.

"You know," said Ruby's dad, "for a dog, you're okay."

Then they went back to watching TV.

Then somewhere in the darkened room, a sigh of relief went out, like a leaf on a breath of wind.

CHAPTER TEN
Cheapo Dad

The good news was that after a few more pet
therapy sessions, Ruby's dad stopped spending so
much time in the bathroom.

He changed his clothes.

He combed his hair.

He shaved his quillery face.

He turned off the TV.

And he started making circles in the classified
ads again.

Then he went out and picked the last of the
fruits from the plum tree. He tied a coat hanger
to the end of an old broom handle to reach the
ones at the very tip-top. And when he was done,

there was a laundry basket full of plums.

"What are we going to do with all these?" asked Ruby excitedly.

"Bake," said Ruby's dad. "We have to bring something to the school Halloween party, don't we?"

"Hooray!" said Ruby. She loved to bake, and she was so happy that her dad was finally in the Halloween mood.

Soon there was flour, sugar, baking soda, salt, and plums everywhere. Especially on Oscar. The house filled with the smell of summer. And even after Ruby and Flying Duck and Oscar sampled a couple dozen of the plum muffins they had made, there were still so many muffins taking up every inch of the kitchen that Ruby and Flying Duck couldn't count them all.

"We'll bring some to school," said Ruby's dad. "And the rest we'll give out on Halloween."

"That's a great idea, Dad!" said Ruby. "We'll be the most popular house on the block!"

Ruby could hardly wait. She forgot all about worrying that they wouldn't have any candy to pass out.

But even better, Ruby's dad agreed to help Ruby and Flying Duck with their costumes.

"It's got to be cheap, cheap, cheap," he warned the girls.

"Cheap, cheap, cheap," chirped Ruby, feeling proud that she had helped her dad come out of his slump.

"Cheap!" peeped Oscar.

"*Owwwwooooo,*" howled Elvis.

Everyone laughed. Even Elvis seemed to like cheap.

But cheap meant ballerinas were out.

Princesses were out.

Queens were out.

Witches were out.

Even ghosts were out.

"Too much fabric," said Ruby's dad, adding hand motions and a little bit of sign language. "And if we cut our old sheets, we can't buy new ones."

Ruby's dad was no fun.

He was cheap.

"Cheap is fun," Ruby's dad assured her and Flying Duck.

"When I was a boy," he said, "my dad was so cheap that instead of rain boots, he'd tie plastic bags around our feet. We carried our shoes to school to avoid ruining them, and then we put them on when we got there."

Ruby and Flying Duck found some plastic bags and tied them around their own feet to see what it was like. It was fantastic! Ruby loved stories about her dad when he was her age.

"When I was a boy," Ruby's dad continued, "my dad was so cheap that we wore backpacks filled with ice in the summer as air-conditioning."

Ruby laughed so hard she forgot that her dad was no fun.

"My dad was so cheap," Ruby's dad added, "we had to refreeze the melted ice to make more air-conditioning."

"How cheap was your dad?" asked Ruby.

"My dad was so cheap," said her dad, "he made musical instruments out of old shoes and Christmas ornaments out of old spools . . . and there wasn't a cardboard box that he didn't like."

"We have cardboard boxes," said Ruby.

Then everyone hurried out to the garage, where Ruby's dad pulled out two gigantic cardboard boxes that he'd been saving for a rainy day.

He fitted one on Ruby.

Then he fitted the other one on Flying Duck.

Next he found some old paint and paintbrushes.

Then he put the girls to work.

They cut and painted and taped and pasted for hours.

By the time they finished, nothing and no one was recognizable.

It wasn't exactly what Ruby had in mind.

It was better.

Much better.

Ruby was a washing machine.

And Flying Duck was a dryer.

And they even had blinking lights for all the different cycles, which were Christmas lights powered by a battery taped inside.

And Oscar, wearing a big plastic jug cut in half, was a bottle of detergent.

"*Oowwwwooo,*" Elvis howled.

"We didn't forget you, Elvis," said Ruby. "You're the laundry dog. You can pull a laundry basket behind you in the parade."

Elvis stuck out his tongue, hopped up on his hind legs, and danced.

This made the washing machine and dryer

laugh and jiggle like a couple of real machines.

And the bottle of detergent laughed so hard, it fell over on its side.

Ruby's dad was right. Cheap was fun. It meant using your imagination instead of your wallet. It could make something out of nothing. And it gave you a costume that no one else would have. Best of all, Ruby now had a cheapo dad story to tell.

"My dad's so cheap," Ruby sang after dinner.

"Cheap, cheap!" echoed Oscar, as they marched around the living room in their costumes.

"He turned me into a washing machine!" sang Ruby. She could hardly wait to see her friends' faces when they saw her and Flying Duck side by side in the Halloween parade.

"My dad's so cheap!" sang Ruby. "He's so cheap, he . . . he . . ." She went through the alphabet in her head to find something that rhymed with cheap. "He can make your machines beep!"

Ruby's dad smiled at her. And Ruby smiled back. She was so proud of her dad.

That was the good news.

The bad news was that all this talk about being cheap made Ruby's dad want to be even cheaper.

"We have to cut back on our expenses," Ruby heard her dad say late that night when she was in bed. Her parents were in the hallway outside Ruby and Flying Duck's room. Every night Ruby would listen for them to pass her room on their way to bed before she would allow herself to fall asleep. The sound of their footsteps and the same questions they asked each other every night ("Is the stove off?" "Are the doors locked?") were as comforting to Ruby as their good-night kisses on her forehead.

"We're already doing all we can, sweetheart," said Ruby's mom.

"Seems to me my parents were able to do with even less," said Ruby's dad. "There must be some way that we can cut back even further...."

"This isn't a contest," said Ruby's mom.

"No," said Ruby's dad. "But we've got taxes to pay next month."

Silence.

"Maybe the dog," said Ruby's dad.

Ruby gasped.

"My dad was so cheap," Ruby's dad continued, "he never allowed us to have a dog."

Ruby could hardly believe her ears.

"How much is dog food every month?" asked her dad. "He eats like a pig. He must be adding quite a bit to our food bill."

Ruby froze.

At the foot of her bed, Elvis lifted his ears.

"Just buy the cheapest dog food you can find," said Ruby's mom.

"It's still an expense," said Ruby's dad. "A dog is a luxury."

"Then we'll feed him leftovers," said Ruby's mom. "I thought you liked Elvis."

"He has grown on me," Ruby's dad admitted. "But we've got those darn taxes. . . ."

"A month's worth of dog food isn't going to pay our taxes," said Ruby's mom.

"Yes, but twelve months' worth . . . ," said her dad, before Ruby's mom cut him off.

"When your ship is sinking, you don't start throwing people overboard," she said. "You do what you can to keep the ship afloat."

Their footsteps stopped.

"Besides," said Ruby's mom, "you know how Ruby feels about that dog. He's a member of our family. We don't get rid of family members when things get rough."

Then Ruby heard no more. Her parents went into their room and shut the door.

Muffled voices came through the walls.

Then silence.

For a while Ruby listened to the night noises of the house. These sounds were comforting to her too. The house was like a good friend that talked to her until she fell asleep. She wished that Flying Duck could hear and fall asleep this way too.

Then Ruby listened to the wind outside. *Shhhhh-hhhhhhh*, said the wind. *Shhhhhhhhhhhhhh.*

Ruby shut her eyes.

She lay very still.

Slowly a tear rolled out of one eye.

Then another tear rolled out of the other.

Then another.

And another.

And another.

Until Ruby drifted away to a safer place.

CHAPTER ELEVEN
Some Dog

This is how to help your dog fly under the radar, another one of Ruby's dad's strange sayings that means the same as keeping a low profile:

1. Sunglasses
2. Trench coat
3. Wig
4. Camouflage
5. Secret weapon
6. Mysterious foreign accent (or bark)
7. Doggy booties (plastic bags tied around his feet)
8. Secret code

With Ruby's help, Elvis was practically invisible. If you could see him, it was easy to mistake him for a secret agent or a lawn ornament. He was camouflaged so well you'd hardly even know he was in the house. And with the booties, he left no tracks.

The only problem was, no matter how well disguised he was, or how many secret code signals Ruby sent, Elvis still ate like a pig.

He ate more than anyone else in the family.

Worse, he had no manners when he ate. He slurped and chomped and slobbered and snorted. Then he'd wolf down the rest. After that he'd beg at the table.

It was not a very secret agent thing to do.

Flying Duck had an idea. She tried to tell Ruby that in China it is common for kids in poor families to help earn money to feed their families. But Ruby didn't understand sign language very well. So Flying Duck did the best she could, making up her own signs and drawing pictures to help Ruby understand that because Elvis was eating too much:

he had to start singing
for his supper:

or else!

"What a great idea!" said Ruby.
"Why didn't I think of it?"

Fortunately, Ruby had seen something on the
Internet that just might help. So they hurried to the
computer.

IS YOUR DOG CUTE? OR TALENTED? OR UNUSUAL? The
words moved across the computer screen.

Ruby looked at Elvis. He was very old. But he
was very gorgeous. His fur was mangy but silky.
His ears were floppy. His teeth, straight. His jaw
was square and strong. There was something very
special about him.

"Yes." Ruby nodded. "All of the above."

THEN POST HIS PICTURE HERE, said the screen. YOUR PET MAY HAVE THE RIGHT TRAINING AND PERSONALITY TO BECOME AN ANIMAL ACTOR OR MODEL.

Ruby clicked and clicked. She had many pictures of Elvis in her computer. Each one was gorgeous and stunning.

"Which one?" she asked Flying Duck.

"Post them all," signed Flying Duck, pointing to the pictures.

So Ruby did. She posted all of them.

"Being well-trained is the most basic requirement of an animal actor," Ruby read slowly and carefully.

Oops. Elvis was not well trained. He had a mind of his own.

"Each additional skill, such as sitting up on his hind legs, chasing his tail, swimming, and doing things on command, makes your pet that much more likely to find work."

"Hmmm," said Ruby.

"Animal actors can earn fifty to four hundred dollars a day," she read.

"Hot dog!" Ruby cried. "If you earned that much, you could eat all you want, *and* pay taxes."

Unfortunately, none of Elvis's talents were on the list.

But fortunately, Ruby remembered another one of her dad's expressions: It's never too late to teach an old dog new tricks. Or was it you *can't* teach an old dog new tricks? Ruby couldn't remember.

"You gotta start doing as I say," Ruby began to tell Elvis. "Or . . . or . . . or my dad will give you away," she finished tearfully, grabbing Elvis and squeezing him close.

"*Oowwwwoooo*," cried Elvis.

"*Waaaaaaaaah*," cried Ruby. "*Waaaaaaaaaah!*"

Elvis didn't have the right skills for anything. No one would ever hire him to be an animal actor or a dog model. He couldn't follow even the simplest direction.

But Ruby was determined to change all that.

"No more fooling around, mister," said Ruby, drying her tears. "We're starting doggy boot camp."

◎

If there was anything good about hard times, it was this: Ruby no longer had to go to Chinese school on Saturdays. It was one of the first expenses her parents cut.

And if there was anything good about not going to Chinese school, it was this: You had the entire day to get your dog into shape.

And if there was anything else good about hard times, it was this: The entire 20th Avenue Plum Club was over to help.

"Sit," said Ruby.

Elvis sprung up on his hind feet and gave her a kiss.

"This is supposed to be boot camp!" cried Ruby, stomping her foot. But it was hard to be a drill sergeant when you'd just been kissed.

So then Emma took a turn. She had graduated from dog obedience school with her own dog and knew exactly how to do it. She looked him smack in the eye and gave him the command.

"Heel," said Emma.

Elvis popped up again and began to twirl on his hind legs, asking Emma for a dance.

It was very charming.

But it wasn't going to pay for his supper.

Then Elvis slid down into his favorite yoga position.

He was a Down Dog.

Then he was a Cobra.

Then he was a Spider.

Then he was a Down Dog again.

"You're some dog," said Ruby, exasperated.

And he was.

Elvis was some dog.

More than that, he was some yoga dog.

He stretched himself out on the lawn and began to do Up Dog . . . when his yoga paw stretched next to something strange under the leaves.

At first Ruby didn't know what it was. It looked like just another leaf underneath all the other leaves. It was green, like a leaf from a different season.

It was not red or brown or yellow like the leaves around it.

But it wasn't a leaf.

It was a little triangle.

And when the leaves lifted and blew aside, the green triangle stuck out of a brown rectangle.

"Oh," said Ruby.

She picked it up. It was a wallet. And the green triangle was the tip of a bill. Inside the wallet, there was a *wad* of bills. In fact, there were so many bills that when Ruby took them out and folded them in half she had a *book* of money.

Ruby flipped it this way.

Then she flipped it that way.

She had never seen so much money before in her entire life. And neither had any of her friends.

"Wow," said Christina. "You're rich."

"I am," said Ruby.

She was very rich. She counted. Then she recounted. Then she counted again.

"I can't count that high," Ruby finally confessed.

So Flying Duck and Christina helped. They were the best counters on 20th Avenue South. And when they finished, they announced that there was $360. Nothing else was in the wallet. No pictures. No credit cards. No library card. Nothing.

Dry leaves swirled like crispy potato chips around their feet.

It was a lot of money. It would probably pay for dog food *and* taxes, whatever they were.

"What are you going to do with it?" asked Tiger.

"Give it to my dad," said Ruby.

It was so easy. Why hadn't she thought of that in the first place? All she had to do was find a wallet. And the worst of their money troubles was over, just like that.

CHAPTER TWELVE
Just Helping Out

This is what *not* to do if you find a wallet and want to save your dog:

> Show it to your dad.
> Hear him gasp.
> Watch him count.
> Hear the other grown-ups gasp.
> Listen to a family conference about finding the owner.
> Help your dad write an ad for the newspaper.

"Found: Wallet," wrote Ruby's dad. "Description necessary for its safe return."

Then he crossed it out.

"Too many words," he muttered.

"Describe it to prove it's yours," suggested Ruby's mom.

Ruby's dad tried it and crossed that out too.

"Prove it's yours," Ruby said.

Her dad paused.

"That's it!" he said. "Perfect!"

"Writing an ad is like writing haiku," said Ruby. "It's hard."

Ruby's dad typed the ad into the computer. Then he clicked the submit button.

"If we don't find the owner this way," said Ruby's dad, "we'll try some other way."

"We will?" asked Ruby. She wobbled like a little bird perched on the chair behind her dad. She didn't want to try some other way. She didn't even want to try this way. It was not her idea. It was her dad's. And it was not a very good one.

"But Elvis is the owner," Ruby said. "Finders keepers."

Silence.

Then Ruby's dad took in a big breath.

"Ruby," he said. "Finders are not keepers. Finders are helpers. We need to find the person who lost this."

"Why?" asked Ruby. "We need the money. You said we don't have enough money for dog food . . . or taxes."

"Oh dear," said Ruby's mom.

"The money is not ours to keep," Flying Duck's mom said in Chinese.

"Always better to return than to keep," added Flying Duck's dad.

Ruby could not believe it. These were the same grown-ups who stayed up late worrying about money. Now that they had some money, they worried about returning it! It made no sense.

The next day Ruby's dad made an announcement in church about the found wallet.

Then he made flyers—with Ruby's help—in the form of a haiku:

> *Found: One men's wallet,*
> *Describe it to prove it's yours,*
> *Eager to return.*

On Monday he passed out the flyers with the plum muffins at the school Halloween party.

This made Ruby's wash cycle lights blink like crazy. She was not pleased that her dad was telling everyone that they had a wallet up for grabs.

Ruby was so busy blinking and glaring at her dad that she couldn't remember marching in the Halloween parade at all.

She missed the pumpkin cupcakes. . . .

She missed bobbing for apples. . . .

She missed the hayride. . . .

She missed the family pictures. . . .

And finally, she almost missed a very important announcement:

"FIRST PLACE FOR BEST COSTUME GOES TO . . .

"RUBY AND FLYING DUCK!"

Ruby stopped.

There was applause.

Cameras flashed.

Blue ribbons were slapped on.

"Congratulations, girls," said Mr. Yu, shaking

their hands. "The vote was unanimous."

Ruby was speechless. And so was Flying Duck.

Then everyone swarmed over to have their picture taken with the washing machine and dryer and the bottle of detergent that kept tipping over and the dog-drawn laundry basket that kept doing yoga.

It was a dream come true!

And if there had been a prize for best baked goods, they would have won that, too. Even the principal came by and declared it a healthy snack. Then she wished Ruby luck in finding the owner of the wallet.

"These are hard times," said Miss Kallianpur. "It shows a lot of character that you want to return it."

Ruby nodded. Her thoughts foamed. Her washing machine rocked back and forth as though it were in the spin cycle. She didn't know what Miss Kallianpur was talking about. Character? Which Chinese character did she mean? Ruby only wished that they could keep the money. And she wished that her dad wouldn't say anything more about it to anyone.

But he was a man on a mission.

After Halloween, Ruby's dad posted a sign at the barbershop where he used to get his hair cut. It was a men's wallet, and most men who lived in the neighborhood got their hair cut there, so the wallet's owner would probably show up sooner or later, he said.

Then he posted the same sign at the grocery store where everyone shopped.

After that, he posted another online notice, just in case.

Days passed.

Then weeks.

Finally, just before Thanksgiving, Ruby's dad divided the money in half. He put half of it in one envelope, and the other half in another envelope.

Then they walked over to Panchito's house. Ruby's dad put one of the envelopes in their mailbox.

Then they marched over to Wally's house. And Ruby's dad put the second envelope in their mailbox.

Ruby's jaw dropped.

"What are you doing, Dad?" she asked, when they turned around to head home.

"Just helping out," he replied. "Their dads have been out of work much longer than I have."

Ruby felt very confused. And she was mad. When they got home, she stomped her foot.

"Why, Dad?" Ruby asked. Tears filled her eyes. "Why did you do that? Don't you want to keep Elvis? Don't you want to buy taxes?"

Ruby's father gathered Ruby into his arms. Tears rolled down her cheeks.

"Elvis isn't going anywhere," said Ruby's dad. "I need my dog therapist, remember?

"And as for why I did that," he whispered, "I don't know why."

Ruby's family didn't even know Panchito's family. No one really knew them. Ruby knew that Panchito was no fun. He didn't like anything. And he'd only recently started hanging out with Ruby's Plum Club.

The next day, Panchito walked into Fred's candy store for the first time.

He bought a giant jawbreaker and a tiny bag of jellybeans.

He had a crinkly little brown bag like everyone else, and the scent of sugar wafted behind him.

Then he stood with the rest of the gang in front of the store and ate his goodies.

No one said anything. The only noise was from the swallowing of chocolate and the snapping of sugar sticks and the crinkling of rice paper wrapper and the scraping of teeth against a gumball.

Panchito worked on his jawbreaker until his tongue and lips and teeth were blue, blue, blue.

"*¡Que rico!*" purred Panchito. "*¡Riquisimo!*"

He liked it. He liked it very much.

CHAPTER THIRTEEN
Jobs Eddy

Around the holidays, stores and restaurants filled with customers and needed to hire extra people. So Flying Duck's mom and dad found jobs in a couple of busy Chinese restaurants.

Neighbors dropped off yummy casseroles, lasagna, and pie at Ruby's house. A turkey appeared too, with all the fixings for a traditional Thanksgiving dinner, including Ruby's favorite—sushi—and cranberry and walnut stuffing. Bags of clothes were also left for the girls, and diapers for Oscar. Doggy treats were left for Elvis. Then winter coats and boots, just the right size, appeared for Ruby and Flying Duck.

"But it's not even Christmas yet," said Ruby.

"Hard times can bring out the best in people," said her mom.

Ruby's head tilted with the thought. For the first time in a long time, her mom was home and her dad was not. They were working on a jigsaw puzzle together with Flying Duck. Oscar was taking a nap, and it was the only time that the little pieces were safe from his reach.

"Is that why Daddy gave all that money away?" Ruby asked.

"I think so," said her mom. "And maybe someone else has made a similar sacrifice so that they could give us something."

Ruby thought about it. She wondered if there was another little girl like her who was mad at her mom or dad for giving away their turkey and stuffing.

"I don't like giving up things," said Ruby, pushing some of the puzzle pieces around. "It's scary."

"It's terrifying," said Ruby's mom. "It takes a lot of bravery to make a sacrifice like that."

Ruby looked at her mom. She didn't look as tired as when she first started working. In fact, something about her mom was different. She seemed to like having a job now. And when she was home, she seemed to enjoy being at home even more than before everything changed.

"Are you that brave, Mom?" asked Ruby.

"I hope so," said Ruby's mom.

"Am I that brave, Mom?" said Ruby.

"I hope so," said Ruby's mom. "I hope you're as brave as your dad."

Ruby nodded. She hoped she was as brave as her dad too. But secretly, she still wished that he hadn't given it all away.

The phone at Ruby's house started ringing for Ruby's dad before Thanksgiving weekend was over.

"Can you fix a washing machine?" someone asked.

"I can try," said Ruby's dad.

"Do you know what to do with a dryer that doesn't work?" asked someone else.

"I'll be glad to take a look for you," said Ruby's dad.

"Have you got a minute?" came another call. "Our cat is stuck up our tree, and I heard that you might have a device to help her down."

"I'll be right there," said Ruby's dad.

Soon word got out that Ruby's dad had many useful skills.

He could get a cat down from a tree by tying a basket to the end of their plum picker.

He could climb a ladder and clean leaves out of the gutter.

He could paint a room.

He could install a wireless network.

He could hook up HDTV.

He could install and fix garage door openers.

And he could bake something in a hurry.

In other words, Ruby's dad was very talented.

So he came up with Plan B.

"I'm now Jobs Eddy," he announced. "No job too hard or too small. You can count on me."

It was great news.

"Does this mean you can buy taxes, Dad?" asked Ruby.

"Yes, Ruby," said her dad. "I can *pay* taxes now."

"And you can buy dog food, too?" asked Ruby.

"Dog food first, taxes second," her dad said, chuckling.

"Yipeee!" cried Ruby, throwing her arms around her dad.

Ruby's mom gave him a hug and a kiss. She said she was very proud of him.

Ruby was very proud of him too. She had the most popular dad in the neighborhood!

"Can I answer your phones for you?" she asked.

"Sure," said her dad.

So the next time the phone rang, Ruby answered.

The voice on the phone said that his dog had run away during the summer. He had nearly given up his search until he found his dog's picture on a dog modeling website.

His dog could be a little ornery, the voice continued. His dog had a mind of his own.

But when his dog was working, he was perfect. He was a circus dog. And he was very, very professional. They belonged in a show together.

"Oh," said Ruby.

There was a long silence.

"Without him," the voice explained, "I don't have a job."

There was another long silence.

"Hello? Hello, is anyone there?"

Click. Ruby hung up.

Maybe it was an accident.

Maybe the phone had just slipped from her hands.

Maybe the man on the other end was driving and the connection was cut off.

Maybe the phone never rang in the first place.

"Ruby?" said Ruby's dad. "Who was that on the phone?"

"No one," said Ruby.

Then the phone rang again.

This time Ruby's dad answered.

"Yes," he said into the phone. "Hmm ... I see. ... Of course. ... Well, that explains a lot of things. ..."

By the time her dad got off the phone, Ruby was in tears.

It was much worse than giving up the wallet.

It was the end of the world.

CHAPTER FOURTEEN
The End of the World

The End of the World was an old man walking down the street.

Ruby could hardly breathe. She watched him from her front window.

Her eyes were as round as chocolate coins as she watched the End of the World get closer and closer.

He didn't look like a dog owner.

He didn't walk like a dog owner.

He didn't look like he knew anything about dogs. He looked quite ordinary. His shoes were old. His hat was old. His coat was old.

In fact, he looked a lot like a certain old dog Ruby knew. . . .

And when the doorbell rang, no one moved. No one dared move. No one, that is, except for Ruby's dad. He answered the door.

And Elvis, who usually hid whenever anyone approached the house, thundered out of nowhere. He barked. He kissed. He whimpered. His tail wagged and wagged. No one on 20th Avenue South had ever seen Elvis so happy.

"That's a good boy, Thunder!" said the man.

Thunder?

"His sister's name is Lightning," said the man. "They work together." Then the man's whole face lit up. He was so happy.

But Ruby was not. A tear rolled down her cheek. She began to cry. She cried and cried. She could not stop.

Ruby felt very, very little. And everything else suddenly felt very, very big.

"You have taken excellent care of Thunder," the man said. "He looks better now than when I was taking care of him."

Ruby nodded.

"This means more to me than you know," said the man. "You deserve a big reward."

The man didn't have any money. So he wrote a check. It read:

Pay to the order of Miss Ruby Lu . . . One hundred dollars

Ruby gasped. It was a lot of money.

"You earned it," said the man. "Without your fine care, I would have had to train another dog . . . then I'd be out of work even longer."

Ruby thought about it. Her family sure could use the money.

Then she handed the check back to the man.

"It's okay," Ruby whispered. "You keep it."

Silence.

"Do you want a larger reward?" the man asked.

"No," said Ruby, choking back tears. "My dad's been out of work too."

The man nodded. Ruby could tell that he loved Thunder and was a good dad to him.

Then Ruby gave Thunder one last hug good-bye, letting her tears roll onto his fur and straight into his heart. If she could have kept Thunder, she would have. She would have kept him forever.

The man bowed.

Thunder bowed.

Then they were gone, just like that.

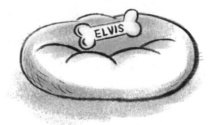

CHAPTER FIFTEEN
Star of the Show

Rain pelted Ruby's windows. The rainy season had arrived.

But when thunder rolled down 20th Avenue South . . . there was a dog-size silence in Ruby's house.

It was hard to like a good storm much anymore.

To make matters worse, there was a dog-size space in Ruby's bed.

And a dog-size hole in Ruby's heart.

Everywhere Ruby looked, everything was dog-size.

Just before Christmas, there came a dog-size letter in Ruby's mailbox. Ruby ripped it open. And this is what she found:

Dear Ruby,
I am sending you free tickets to see me at the circus. Please bring your family and friends. You will be our honored guests. There will be a surprise. My dad thinks you will enjoy it. I miss you.
Love,

Ruby was very impressed.

She showed it to all her friends.

They read the letter. They inspected the tickets. No one on 20th Avenue South had ever been to the circus.

But everyone had read the posters. They'd seen the commercials.

"Hot dog!" Wally said. "Genuine circus tickets!"

"I like the circus!"

added Panchito, who was beginning to like a lot of things now.

Finally Ruby showed it to her dad.

He read the letter. He inspected the tickets. He looked at the front of the letter. Then he looked at the back of it. He sniffed the ink. He studied the signature. He held each ticket close, then far away.

Ruby held her breath.

Her dad was as quiet as pajamas.

Finally he said, "I'd always suspected he could write."

Family Night at the circus was magical.

"HURRY! HURRY! HURRY!"

"STEP RIGHT UP!"

"GET YOUR PROGRAM HERE!"

"GET YOUR POPCORN HERE!"

Ruby hurried, hurried, hurried.

Balloons floated by.

A fairy on stilts ambled past.

Clowns poked one another.

Panchito's mother stopped a cotton candy

man and bought a fluffy pink bouquet.

Christina's mom took pictures.

Wally's dad treated his family to popcorn.

Tiger's mom kept saying it was the most fun she'd had in a long time.

Oscar and Emma's baby brother, Sam, looked like seven-foot-tall babies in the Hall of Mirrors.

And Ruby's parents were smiling and holding hands and pointing at all the bright and colorful sights.

By the time they made it to their seats, Ruby and her friends were bursting with excitement.

"WELCOME . . . LADIES AND GENTLEMEN . . . BOYS AND GIRLS . . . TO ANIMALS ON HOLIDAY!" a voice boomed from the loudspeakers. "THE WORLD'S MOST UNUSUAL TALENTS!"

Then . . . monkeys played basketball.

Raccoons twirled batons.

Squirrels cracked nuts in time
to the Blue Danube waltz.

Pigs flew in the air.

Ruby was completely and utterly transfixed.
And so was everyone else. The audience clapped
and clapped.

Then it got quiet. Drums rolled.
Ruby held her breath. It was the
moment she had been waiting
for. . . .

"LADIES AND GENTLEMEN,
THE WORLD'S MOST AMAZING DOGS—
THUNDER! AND HIS SISTER, LIGHTNING!"

Thunder and Lightning played cards.

They did yoga.

They played the piano and howled.

They rode bicycles.

They balanced plates and fruit on their heads.

They were very talented.

Ruby clapped and clapped and clapped.

Then suddenly Thunder leaped into the audience.

Everyone gasped.

"Hoooooowwwwrrrrr!" Thunder howled.

He landed right next to Ruby. Then he started kissing her.

The audience laughed.

"Ladies and gentlemen, boys and girls," said the announcer's voice. "It gives me great pleasure to introduce you to MISS RUBY LU."

Ruby blinked. Her eyelashes looked like spider legs in the spotlight. And the light made her skin very warm.

She was being introduced?

"This young lady found Thunder when he ran away," the announcer continued.

Ruby blinked again.

"She took care of him for nearly six months," he continued. "Without her, Lightning and I would no longer be part of the show."

The audience clapped.

"It was very hard for Ruby to give him back to me," said the announcer.

The audience fell silent.

Ruby felt the dog-size hole in her heart. Then she burst out, "IT WAS THE HARDEST THING I'VE EVER HAD TO DO IN MY LIFE!"

Heads nodded.

"Ruby and her family and friends are here tonight because they are the REAL STARS OF THE SHOW!" boomed the announcer's voice.

A drum rolled. Lights crisscrossed the audience. The audience thundered with applause. Then the band began to play.

The announcer helped Ruby into the center ring.

He gave her a helmet, then strapped her on a bicycle built for two with Thunder and Lightning! They pedaled a victory lap around the ring.

The audience went wild.

Ruby was the Star of the Show.

She waved and waved.

She blew kisses.

Best of all . . . being in the circus was just as Ruby imagined—it was as wonderful as being on 20th Avenue South.